MIND *in* FRAGMENTS

A BOOK BY DR AKSHATA

BlueRose ONE.com
Stories Matter
NewDelhi • London

BLUEROSE PUBLISHERS
India | U.K.

For permissions requests or inquiries regarding this publication, please contact:

BLUEROSE PUBLISHERS
www.BlueRoseONE.com
info@bluerosepublishers.com
+91 8882 898 898
+4407342408967

ISBN: 978-93-7542-184-9

Cover Design: Shivam Gaur
Typesetting: Sagar

First Edition: March 2026

CONTENTS

NATURE AS A HEALER

Somewhere far from crowd, people, the noise of traffic.... Lies a home for mental well being exists in nature... Vibing with the music of chirping of birds, an extra add on to it comes from a soothing breeze of those long densely grown forest trees....connecting mentally physically to the nature....Expressing out loud through mind with no words uttered from mouth just calming the disturbed mind with fluttering thoughts of self doubt, low confidence, self questioning, fear of future, traumas of past, just nature helping to keep them in oblivion and making them aloof from the present life and moment...Helping heal the damaged neurons of mind and providing energy to the nerves with the calmness and message it is carrying around it....Before looking into the world looking into self is important being taught by nature...Helping me grow and giving me the energy to learn to live in the present with the satisfaction with having no regrets of past and anxious thoughts of future....Rather than learning to live life as destined to learning to live as I wanted to live it....with zero expectations, and a lot of acceptance comes from lessons learnt that were taught by nature...

FOR SPECIAL ONE

Love, the sculptor of the soul,
A tender force that makes us whole.
It molds our hearts, it bends our will,
Transforms our world, our dreams fulfill.

In its embrace, we lose our fears,
And shed the weight of countless years.
It paints the skies in colors bright,
Turns darkest night to softest light.

Through love, the heart learns to forgive,
And in its warmth, we truly live.
It teaches us to care and share,
And shows us how to deeply care.

Love, it changes, molds, and heals,
Reveals the truth that time conceals.
In every touch, in every glance,
It writes the story of romance.

So yes, love changes all we are,
It turns our wounds to shining stars.
And in its wake, we find anew,
A better self, a truer view.

SOMETIMES

Sometimes it's better to stay quite, sometimes it's better to speak, sometimes it's better to hold on, sometimes it's better to move on, sometimes it's better to be alone, sometimes it's better to be with people around but most of times we get juggled between these thoughts but sometimes we have been made peace with it sometimes we miss, sometimes we would have moved on, sometimes it's better to write, sometimes it's better to read, sometimes it's better to work, sometimes it's better to stay at home, sometimes it's better to have friends, sometimes it's better to be a loner...... A lot can be thought about this but at times it's better to keep these thoughts with us... No matter What it is but it's always good to delve in to our own minds and swim through our own thoughts facing every emotion may be right or wrong trying to understand them or at times better leaving where they are just like that not always somethings need to be told at times somethings some thoughts better left unfurled ....

EFFORTS MATTER

Efforts are meaningful when someone loves you enough to make small adjustments in their life to include you, The sacrifices they make to ensure your happiness and well-being hold more value than anything else in a relationship. When two people truly care for each other, the willingness to alter personal preferences for the sake of the other person speaks volumes. It's these acts of consideration and change that truly matter, showing love in its purest form. Such efforts deepen affection and create a bond that transcends superficial gestures, proving that love includes little things shared between them.

FOR HIM

From waiting to ask him to marry me I saw him getting married to someone else and having family which I wanted to build with him watching him making a home with someone else did shatter my heart down but nevertheless the love for him still remained same... By seeing me grow old with his memories while him growing old with family he had made for one day When his daughter asks him What love is I hope he would be telling about me.. To love with no expectations, no boundaries, no fear of losing, just being happy accepting the fact of our loved one being caught in the arms of others and still wishing them to be happy and successful is real love..him explaining the meaning of real ove without even taking my name but through his actions YES he would be still talking about me

WHAT IS LOVE?

Love is a powerful, multifaceted emotion that connects people in deep, meaningful ways. It encompasses affection, trust, and a sense of belonging, often leading to selflessness and sacrifice. Love can be romantic, familial, or platonic, each form unique but equally vital in shaping human relationships. It fosters empathy, understanding, and support, allowing individuals to grow emotionally and spiritually. Love also brings joy and comfort in times of hardship, creating resilience through connection. At its core, love is a force that transcends differences, heals wounds, and creates lasting bonds, making life more meaningful and enriching for those who experience it.

TO UNGREATFUL WORLD

It's disheartening when our efforts go unnoticed, especially by those We support selflessly. People can become so accustomed to receiving hclp that thcy takc it for granted, failing to appreciate the sacrifices made for them. When the support stops, they may suddenly realize its value, but often it's too late. Those who once gave freely might have moved on, recognizing their efforts were unreciprocated. This situation underscores the importance of mutual respect and acknowledgment in relationships. True gratitude should be expressed regularly, as neglect can lead to lasting rifts and the loss of those who enrich our lives.

A LIGHT IN THE QUITE

In the quiet moments the day,
When shadows drift and softly sway,
You came into my world so bright,
A beacon in the darkest night.
With open heart and gentle grace,
You've seen beyond the outer face,
Understanding in your every glance,
A trust that's grown from circumstance,
n the maze of thoughts where doubts reside,
You've walked with me, right by my side,
Your faith a light that guides my way,
Turning night to hopeful day.
So here's a thanks, from deep within,
For the love and trust you've given,
For seeing me through eyes so true,
And making all my dreams come true.

TRAVELING MOMENTS

Every time I peep through the bars secured windows I see the free nature, free birds flying all over the limitless sky.. And what's stopping me from flying like that, when I questioned myself why can't I just jump out of the moving train and get along with those birds but then I realize Freedom and Independence comes with restrictions....we can still be happy behind the bars but only when we start appreciating the life held within it.... Thats how acceptance starts, life grows, and then we become limitless in the environment we are surrounded that's a life everyone has to learn to live...

BROKEN

The heart aches with an overwhelming pain, a heaviness that refuses to leave. It yearns to speak, to find a way to express the turmoil inside, but the words refuse to come. The mouth remains locked, unable to convey the depth of sorrow, leaving the heart to carry its burden in silence. Each beat echoes the weight of unspoken emotions, and the quiet desperation grows louder. The heart wants to scream, to release the torment, but it feels trapped within itself, unable to find the freedom of expression. The pain lingers, unchecked and raw, as the lips stay tight, suppressing the truth. In this silence, the heart is broken even further, unable to heal because its suffering remains hidden. It's as if the very act of speaking would unravel something fragile, and so, the heart endures in solitude, carrying the weight of unvoiced grief.

SELF LOVE

Self-love is often regarded as the highest form of love because it lays the foundation for all other relationships. When you truly love yourself, you embrace your worth and accept your flaws, which cultivates a deep sense of inner peace and fulfillment. This self-acceptance enables you to set healthy boundaries, make choices that align with your values, and pursue your passions with confidence. Furthermore, self-love fosters resilience, allowing you to handle challenges with grace and optimism. By nurturing yourself, you create a positive self-image that attracts similar respect and kindness from others. This internal stability radiates outward, enhancing your interactions and connections with those around you. Ultimately, self-love is not just about pampering oneself but about recognizing and honoring your intrinsic value, leading to a more authentic and satisfying life. It is the bedrock upon which genuine happiness and meaningful relationships are built.

LONER POWER

Being a loner wasn't my choice, but it became an unavoidable reality. With few options available, I had to embrace solitude and make the best of it. In the quiet of my own company, I discovered the strength to enjoy my own solace and delve deeper into self-understanding. Solitude, once a burden, transformed into a sanctuary for personal growth. Through reflection and introspection, I began to appreciate my own presence and found clarity in my thoughts. This journey of self-discovery, though solitary, revealed a profound connection with myself that I might never have found amidst the clamor of constant companionship.

TRUST AGAIN

Once the heart is broken because of betrayals, false promises, fake love and so on....The reasons may be many.. But eventually we learn to rebuild what's broken with self love, self confidence and by self prioritising ...but it's just not about rebuilding ....when something is rebuilt it always comes with some scars...The scars may be of many kinds like trust deficit, being left alone again, pistanthrophobia and many more... In these juggling thoughts we fear to love again fear to share feelings afraid to handover the rebuilt heart to other person... But if you hold on to it forever you will never know who would be able to take care of it.. Yes there will be many Chances of it getting broken again but when you have mastered the art of rebuilding then why fear of getting broken.... Isn't it!!??

ABSENCE

In the absence of his presence each passing moment is a symphony.. is in this crucial note leaving the melody incomplete...Memories, like fragments of shattered mosaic, whisper reminders of his laughter, his warmth, his essence interwinded with mine...gaze held with unspoken words of endless feelings for him penned down in this note..feels like cherished treasures locked away in this vault of time..

His absence casts a shadow that colors every experience, every joy, every thought reminding him of the void left behind...It's a bitter sweet symphony....Though the pain persists , it also stands as a tribute to profound love and connection I once held for him, A love that continues to shape and color my world even in his absence...

LONELY

There are times when loneliness feels unbearable — when your heart is overflowing with things you want to say, but you don't know where to begin, who to trust, or if anyone will truly listen. You wonder, Will they understand? Or will they walk away like everyone else?

All we really hope for is that someone, just once, chooses to stay. Chooses to fight for us.Because we're not unlovable — we just love deeply, fully, without holding back. That's not a weakness; it's who we are.But when you give someone your everything, and they still let you down, it hurts in ways words can't explain. The betrayal cuts deeper because your intentions were pure.Still, it's not about loving less — it's about finding someone who sees that love, values it, and holds it with care. Until then, protect your heart, but don't change it.

ACKNOWLEDGMENT OF MISTAKE

When a person acknowledges their mistake, they reclaim their power. Admitting fault is an act of courage, demonstrating self-awareness and responsibility. This removes any control others might have over them, as it denies the chance for manipulation or blame. Those who seek to harm or destroy lose their leverage when the individual embraces accountability. Rather than reacting defensively or hiding, the person owning their mistake stands strong, refusing to be defined by past errors. In doing so, they regain their integrity and inner strength, transforming potential weakness into a powerful force for growth and resilience.

POWER OF SUCCESS

When you achieve success, society tends to overlook your marital status, focusing instead on the stature you've built for yourself. Success speaks louder than any label—whether single, married, or otherwise. It's your accomplishments, your influence, and your ability to impact others that shape how you're perceived. In the end, it's the mark you leave on the world that defines your true status, not your relationship status.

POWER OF SELF RELIANCE

There are moments in life when it's important to face your battles alone. While support from others can be valuable, learning to stand on your own teaches you more than any external help ever could. When you confront challenges independently, you begin to recognize your personal strengths and understand your limitations. This self-awareness is crucial because it allows you to grow, improve, and evolve without constantly relying on others.

Self-reliance builds resilience. It teaches you how to manage adversity, make decisions with confidence, and trust your instincts. Over time, this independence fosters a sense of inner strength that becomes unshakable. You no longer seek validation or approval from others because you know your worth. This shift in mindset brings a deep sense of confidence and fearlessness that empowers every aspect of your life.

The journey toward self-reliance isn't always easy. It requires courage, patience, and persistence. But the rewards are immeasurable. Once you realize that you can navigate life on your own, you're free—free from fear, free from dependency, and free to live authentically. You begin to make choices that align with your true self rather than trying to fit into someone else's expectations.

Ultimately, learning to fight your own battles is about discovering who you really are. It's a powerful reminder that you are capable, strong, and enough. And once you understand this, you carry a strength within that no one can take away.

RESET AND RISE AGAIN

Life doesn't always go as planned, and sometimes things fall apart. But no matter how broken the past may seem, you always have the power to start fresh. Hit reset. Take control of your life again. It's okay if you've stumbled or lost your way—what matters now is how you rise from it.

Everyone faces setbacks, but not everyone chooses to fight back. Standing up after a fall takes strength, and that strength is what sets true winners apart. The world may offer sympathy to those who give up, but it celebrates those who rise, rebuild, and refuse to be defeated. These are the people who earn respect, admiration, and love—not because their lives were perfect, but because they had the courage to keep going.

This is your reminder that it's never too late. You are not your past. You are the choices you make today. Help yourself. Believe in your ability to change the course of your life. Start with one step, then another. Progress may be slow, but every effort counts. The power to transform your story lies within you—own it, live it, and rise to become everything you were meant to be.

REDEFINING WHAT IT MEANS TO WIN

Failure is often seen as something negative—a sign that you weren't good enough or didn't try hard enough. But in truth, failure can be one of the greatest wins in life. When relationships end, friendships fade, or you fall short in academics or career goals, it's not always a loss. Sometimes, it's life's way of clearing the path for something better. The people who leave your life may not have been meant to stay. The opportunities that slipped away may not have been right for you. And that's okay.

Real growth comes when you stop measuring your worth by external achievements and start embracing your journey. The real winner isn't the one who never falls, but the one who isn't afraid to fall—and more importantly, isn't afraid to rise again. Life is full of second chances, new connections, and unexpected opportunities. You just have to be open to see them.

Don't waste your energy mourning what's gone. Crying over lost projects, failed relationships, or missed ranks only holds you back. Instead, focus on the lessons learned, the resilience you've built, and the new doors waiting to open. Every setback is a setup for a stronger comeback.

In the end, winning isn't about always coming first—it's about staying in the game, learning from the losses, and never giving up on yourself. That mindset is what truly defines success.

STORM LOVE

You came like thunder—loud, alive,
A flash of light, my soul revived.
At first, your winds were soft and kind,
A wildness I had longed to find.

I opened doors, I let you in,
No fear of loss, no thought of sin.
I gave you skies without a cloud,
A love so deep, so pure, so proud.

But storms don't stay—they roll and break,
And in their wake, the heart will ache.
You left me empty, torn in two,
Yet still, I couldn't let go of you.

For I have loved storms all my days—
Their fierce, unyielding, ruthless ways.

And though you took more than you gave,
I smiled while drowning in your wave.

I wish you joy, where'er you roam,
A warmth, a love, a truer home.
The kind I couldn't give to you,
Though everything I gave was true.

No boundaries drawn, no lines to keep,
Just silent prayers I whisper deep.
They say the world craves love like mine—
But only in a tale, a rhyme.

In truth, they fear what cannot bend,
A love that burns, with no pretend.
Yet still I choose to live that way,
To give, not ask, come what may.

So let the world call me naïve,
I'll keep the faith, I still believe.
For storms may go, and hearts may break,
But real love gives, and does not take.